AF506183

Titles in This Series:

Jungle Babies
Farm Friends
Pets, Pets, Pets
Little Birds, Big Birds

Jungle Babies

Text by Henry Mangione
Illustrations by Nemo

A Little Simon Book

Published by Simon & Schuster, Inc.
New York

Created and manufactured by arrangement with Ottenheimer Publishers, Inc.
Copyright © 1987 by Ottenheimer Publishers, Inc.
All rights reserved including the right of reproduction in whole or in part in any form.
Published by LITTLE SIMON, a division of Simon & Schuster, Inc.,
Simon & Schuster Building, 1230 Avenue of the Americas, New York, New York 10020.
LITTLE SIMON and colophon are trademarks of Simon & Schuster, Inc.
Manufactured in Hong Kong.
10 9 8 7 6 5 4 3 2 1
ISBN 0-671-63488-7

Black Panther

The black panther is also known as a black leopard. That's because it's really nothing more than a leopard whose fur is black all over, instead of spotted. Although panthers are smaller than lions or tigers, they are very fierce fighters and excellent hunters.

Baby panthers are born and raised in the rough rocks deep in the jungle. Their mothers teach them everything they need to know about hunting. They learn how to sneak up on animals, which direction they should attack from, how to hide, and how to attack without scaring their prey. Panther cubs practice pouncing on each other when they are babies. After a while the cubs can hunt well enough to find a territory and have families of their own.

African Elephant

The elephant is the heaviest land animal on earth. When a baby elephant is born, the whole herd helps. When baby elephants are born, they weigh 250 pounds. Grown-up elephants can weigh nearly six tons. That is twelve thousand pounds.

African elephants have very large ears. They have no hair, except on their tail. Elephants are always wearing their teeth down by eating rough food. They live up to 60 years and go through six sets of teeth. Elephant tusks are really giant teeth that elephants can use as weapons, or to dig up trees.

Elephants cannot see well, but their sense of smell is excellent. They can also learn to do simple tricks, the way circus elephants do. Elephants use their trunks the same way people use their arms. They bring food to their mouths, pick things up, and even give themselves showers.

Indian Rhinoceros

The Indian rhinoceros likes to live near the water. It likes to go deep under water where pesky bugs can't bite. Tick birds are good friends of the rhino because they eat ticks and other bugs right off the rhino's skin!

Rhinoceros horns are not made of bone, but of tightly packed hair. Even though they look clumsy, rhinos can run very fast. Rhinos take very good care of their young. When baby rhinos are born, they have pink skin and no horns.

A rhinoceros is a good fighter, but is only dangerous if it is bothered. What the rhino likes best is eating, sleeping, and bathing.

Orangutan

Orangutans take extra good care of their children. The mothers clean their babies' fur with rainwater, carry them everywhere, and even chew their food up first. Orangutan babies, just like human babies, like to eat soft, mushy food.

Orangutans are a lot like people. Their name means 'man of the woods'. Their skin is greyish brown, and they have rust-colored fur. Orangutans' arms are so long that they touch the ground even when they stand up. Orangutans can swing from tree to tree in the jungle and they eat only plants, flowers, and fruit. Their homes are in nests high up in the trees. Since they often weigh over 200 pounds, orangutans check each branch carefully before stepping on it.

Tiger

The tiger is the largest member of the cat family.
Tigers live in jungles and in icy cold places, too. The
very largest tigers are from Siberia. Tigers from warm
areas are yellow with black stripes, but the Siberian
tiger's coat is grey. All baby tigers are born with thick
fur, but jungle tigers lose this as they get older.

Tiger cubs are born in carefully hidden lairs. Their
mothers care for them and give them milk until they
can eat meat. A mother tiger will fight to the death to
protect her babies. When tiger babies are six months
old, they start learning how to hunt. Their first prey is
birds and young pigs, but adult tigers will eat
anything from insects to young elephants.

Grant's Zebra

Grant's zebras are very careful animals. They have very good hearing and will run away at even the smallest noise. When they are frightened, zebras will run away from the danger as a herd. This is called a stampede.

Grant's zebras look a lot like young horses, but smaller. Zebras cannot be tamed. Grant's zebras have wider stripes than other zebras and these cover their whole bodies. Zebras use camouflage to protect themselves from attack. If zebras keep still, their stripes blend in with the grass and protect them from enemies. At night zebras are almost impossible to see because their coats hide them in shadow.

Lion

The lion is known as The King of the Jungle, but these fierce animals like to spend most of their time sleeping. Lion cubs are born with their eyes open, and their fur is spotted. Though the lionesses usually hunt for the whole family, the father lions bring home the food when the cubs are young. The mothers teach the cubs to hunt until they are about two years old. When lions are five they are full grown.

Male lions may weigh over 500 pounds. Males have manes of fur around their necks, but females do not.

Lions live in groups called prides, but they often fight with each other, especially over food. Lions hunt zebras, gazelle, and other plains animals. They hunt by hiding quietly near the water holes where these animals come to drink. The food is shared by the whole pride.

Cheetah

Cheetahs are the fastest animals on earth. For short distances they can run seventy miles per hour!

When cheetah cubs are born their fur is very dark, but adults are golden tan and have spots like leopards. Adult cheetahs have slender bodies that are about seven or eight feet long from tip to tip.

Young cheetahs are taught how to catch food by their parents. Cheetahs do not hide and stalk prey the way lions do. They run after their food, and then knock it to the ground.

Long ago, cheetahs were tamed and used by kings much the way hunting dogs are used today.

Chimpanzee

Chimpanzees are very smart animals. They have a special chimpanzee language of 30 words that they use to talk together. Young chimps spend their time learning words and playing, just like human children. Young chimps like to eat fruit and play tricks, but they are scared of thunder and storms. They are also very good at copying sounds they hear.

Chimpanzees have long arms and short legs. They can walk on either one, two, or four legs if they prefer. They also like to hang in trees. Each evening, the chimps weave nest-beds made of branches. The bed takes only minutes to make and is only used once. The next night, each chimp builds a new bed for itself.

Giraffe

   Giraffes are the tallest animals in the world. They live on the African grasslands and like to eat the leaves of tall trees. Giraffes have tongues which are 18 inches long. Giraffes can see, smell, and hear very well and are fast runners.

   Baby giraffes are six feet tall when they are born and grow to be 18 feet high! They have split hooves, and little horns on the tops of their heads. Young giraffes like to wrestle with each other.

   Giraffes use camouflage to help protect them from attackers. The giraffes' colors blend in with trees and help to protect them from lions. In the shadows on a sunny day, they are almost invisible!

Leopard

Leopards are the third largest member of the cat family. Male leopards can weigh up to 300 pounds. Their coats are golden tan with lots of black spots. Leopards live in rocklands and in jungles, and they like to climb trees. They often bring their food up in the branches to eat.

Leopards can hunt by day or night. They will eat almost anything from crabs to zebras.

Leopard cubs learn to hunt as soon as they can walk. By the time the cubs are a year old, they are ready to go off and start families of their own.

Jaguar

The jaguar is the largest member of the cat family found in North or South America. Jaguars will eat almost any animal, no matter how small or how big. They will even eat horses and cows.

Young jaguars are taught to move around in trees and how to hunt. They spend most of their time hiding in the trees or hunting for food. When they are seven months old, young jaguars will begin to hunt large animals like pigs and deer.

Jaguars often hunt as a family. They will walk a long way in search of food. When the cubs are old enough, they start to hunt alone.